A NORTH-SOUTH PAPERBACK

NORTH-SOUTH BOOKS
New York / London

MAX AND MOLLY

AND THE
Mystery of
the Missing Honey

WRITTEN AND ILLUSTRATED BY

JÜRG OBRIST

Translated by Rosemary Lanning

Hardcover edition first published in the United States, Great Britain,
Canada, Australia, and New Zealand in 2000 by North-South Books,
an imprint of Nord-Süd Verlag AG, Gossau Zürich, Switzerland.
Originally published in the United States and Canada
in a different form by G. P. Putnam's Sons.
First paperback edition published in 2001.

Copyright © 1989, 2000 by Nord-Süd Verlag AG, Gossau Zürich, Switzerland
First published in Switzerland under the title Max und Molli: Großvater und der Honigdieb
English translation copyright © 2000 by North-South Books Inc.

Distributed in the United States by North-South Books Inc., New York.

Library of Congress Cataloging-in-Publication Data
Obrist, Jürg
[Max und Molli. English]
Max and Molly and the mystery of the missing honey / written and illustrated
by Jürg Obrist; translated by Rosemary Lanning.
p.   cm.
Summary: Max and Molly must find the real thief when Grandpa
suspects them of stealing jars of his freshly made honey.
[1. Grandfathers—Fiction. 2. Bears—Fiction. 3. Honey—Fiction.
4. Mystery and detective stories.] I. Lanning, Rosemary. II. Title.
PZ7.O14Me2000
[E]—dc21   99-56593

A CIP catalogue record for this book
is available from The British Library.

ISBN 0-7358-1266-7 (TRADE BINDING)
1 3 5 7 9 TB 10 8 6 4 2
ISBN 0-7358-1267-5 (LIBRARY BINDING)
1 3 5 7 9 LB 10 8 6 4 2
ISBN 0-7358-1414-7 (PAPERBACK)
1 3 5 7 9 PB 10 8 6 4 2
Printed in Belgium

For more information about our books,
and the authors and artists who create them,
visit our web site: www.northsouth.com

Max and Molly got off the train.
"Hello, Grandpa!" they called.
"Here you are at last," said Grandpa,
looking pleased.

Max and Molly visited their grandpa's house every August. What a wonderful time they always had there!

6

Grandpa knew lots of games to play,
things to do, places to go,

and other bear cubs to invite along for the
fun.

He was the best grandfather in the world.

But this year Grandpa had a new
hobby—bee-keeping.

One morning Max and Molly found Grandpa outside the back door, studying his beehives.

He was totally involved and didn't even notice them. "It's finally time," he said to himself. "Time to make the honey!"

Soon Grandpa's kitchen looked like a laboratory. Grandpa mixed and stirred and cooked his honey for hours and hours.

There were jars everywhere. Jars with light honey, jars with dark honey, jars with thick honey, and jars with runny honey.

"It takes a lot of patience and skill to make honey as good as mine," he told Max and Molly.

Grandpa thought about honey all day long. And at night he dreamed of honey.

Worst of all, Grandpa made Max and
Molly help. They had the most boring
jobs to do.

"It's not fair!" Max and Molly grumbled.
"We have to keep washing jars and
 shooing away the
flies while everyone
else is having fun."

Honey here, honey there, honey everywhere. But Max and Molly were only allowed to taste one tiny spoonful each.

"Unbearable," moaned Max.

"Patience," said Grandpa. "Honey needs time to sit and ripen before it tastes really good."

"Ha!" said Molly. "It will get old and stale."

"What a waste!" said Max with a sigh.

Finally the last jar was filled.

"Aah. Such a beautiful golden shimmer. Outstanding!" Grandpa declared proudly.

He carefully put the jars in the kitchen cupboard.

"Hooray!" cried Max and Molly. "Now we can have some fun tomorrow, right, Grandpa?"

But would you bee-lieve it? The next
morning they discovered something
terrible. One of Grandpa's precious jars
of honey was missing!

"Robbers! Thieves!" shouted Grandpa.
"Someone has stolen my honey!"

Was it the postman? Was it the lady
next door? Or was it . . .

Grandpa looked suspiciously at Max and
Molly.

Who could it be? And how had the thief
done it? Grandpa searched for clues all
day. He was still searching that night.

Before he went to bed, Grandpa locked
the kitchen cupboard and hid the key in
the tin full of bear biscuits.

24

And just to be sure, he pushed the chest
of drawers against the front door.

"That should do it," he said.

The next morning Grandpa almost
fainted from shock. The kitchen cupboard
was wide open! Another jar of honey was
missing!

"Who is this crafty thief?" Grandpa
shouted. "It has to be someone who knew
where I hid the key." He stared hard at
Max and Molly.

"But, Grandpa, we don't have anything
to do with this sticky honey business,"
Max and Molly protested.

It was no use. Grandpa had made up
his mind. He hardly spoke to Max and
Molly all day. Then he sent them to bed
early and without any supper.

"We've got to do something," Max said
to Molly. "We must try to catch the thief
ourselves."

So as soon as they heard Grandpa
snoring, they tiptoed downstairs to the
kitchen . . .

and scattered flour on the floor.

"Come on, let's hide and see what happens," whispered Molly.

They waited and waited. . . .

Suddenly they heard footsteps. A shadow moved along the wall. Max and Molly held their breath.

Would you bee-lieve it?
Grandpa was walking in his sleep!

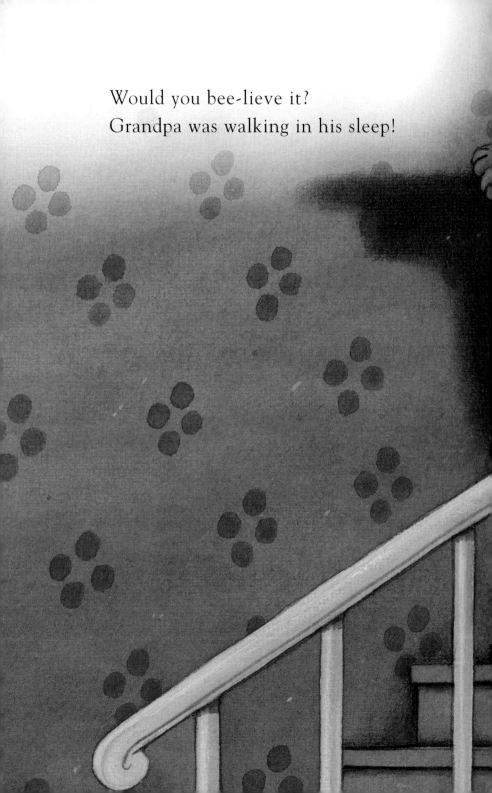

He headed straight for the tin of bear biscuits and one, two, three, he took out the key.

Then he made a beeline for the kitchen
cupboard, unlocked it, and picked up a jar
of honey.

Grandpa carried the jar upstairs to
his bedroom. There he gobbled up the
honey—just as he must have done for
the past two nights.

The next morning Grandpa discovered
that another of his jars of honey was
missing.

"That does it!" he shouted. He was so
angry that his ears trembled and his nose
swelled up.

"Max and Molly, pack your things at once!" he yelled. "I'm sending you home!"

But Max and Molly just smiled. They pointed to Grandpa's big footprints all over the kitchen floor.

They showed Grandpa the three empty honey jars under his bed.

"You are the honey thief, Grandpa!" said Molly.

"You ate the honey in your sleep and thought it was just a sweet dream," said Max.

Grandfather scratched his ear.

"My, oh, my!" he stuttered. "I really did get carried away over the missing honey. I even blamed you, my dear, clever grandchildren! And I was the thief all along. I am so sorry. But I'll make it up to you, I promise."

Molly giggled.

Grandfather chuckled.

Then they all burst out laughing.

"Let's go and have some fun," said
Grandpa.

That evening after supper, Grandpa went
to the kitchen cupboard and took out three
jars of honey—one for each of them.

"Let's all have as much honey as we
want," he said.

"Hooray, hooray!" cried Max and Molly.
And then they sang a song:

"Oh honey, honey, honey,
sticky, fresh, and runny.
It's the best thing to eat,
because it is so sweet.
Grandpa's golden honey
feels yummy in your tummy!"

ABOUT THE AUTHOR/ILLUSTRATOR

Jürg Obrist was born in Zürich, Switzerland. He studied photography there, and then went to the United States, where he taught photography to children and later worked as an illustrator of children's magazines in New York City. He has written and illustrated numerous children's books, and has won many awards, including the Bratislava Book Fair gold medal in 1997. Jürg Obrist once again lives in Zürich.